Lola
the Fashion Show
Fairy

For Lilijana McPherson with lots of love

Special thanks to Sue Mongredien

ISBN 978-0-545-48490-9

12 11 10 9 8 7 6 5 4   13 14 15 16 17 18/0

Printed in the U.S.A.   40

This edition first printing, July 2013

Lola
the Fashion Show
Fairy

by Daisy Meadows

SCHOLASTIC INC.

The
Fairyland
Palace

Tippington
Fountains
SHOPPING CENTER

Top Hats & Tiaras

FASHION

HARTLEYS

Ice Blue
Hair Salon

Fashion Show

TIPPINGTON TOYS

Ice Blue
booth

I'm the king of designer fashion,
Looking stylish is my passion.
Ice Blue's the name of my fashion line,
The designs are fabulous and they're all mine!

Some people think my clothes are odd,
But I will get the fashion world's nod.
Fashion Fairy magic will make my dream come true —
Soon everyone will wear Ice Blue!

Contents

Off to the Show

Kirsty Tate was *very* excited. Today, she and her best friend, Rachel Walker, were going to be in a fashion show! Not only that, but they would be wearing outfits they had designed and made themselves, after entering a special competition held at Tippington Fountains Shopping Center earlier that week.

"I hope I don't trip on the catwalk." Rachel giggled as she, Kirsty, and her parents walked to their meeting place in the mall. "Knowing me, I'll fall flat on my face and totally embarrass myself."

"No, you won't," Kirsty reassured her, squeezing her hand. "You'll be fabulous. And everyone will love your rainbow jeans, I just know it."

Rachel smiled at her. "I'm so glad we're doing this together," she said.

"Me, too." Kirsty grinned. "All of our best adventures happen when we're together, don't they?"

The two girls exchanged a look, their eyes sparkling. No one else knew that they shared an amazing secret. They were friends with the fairies, and they had enjoyed lots of wonderful, magical fairy adventures. Sometimes, the girls had even been turned into fairies themselves, and had been able to fly!

This week, Kirsty was staying with Rachel's family for fall break. Once again, the two friends had found themselves magically whisked away to Fairyland when a brand-new fairy adventure began! They'd been invited to see a fairy fashion show, but it had unfortunately been hijacked by Jack Frost. He and his goblins had barged in, all wearing outfits from Jack Frost's new designer label, Ice Blue. Jack Frost had declared that everyone should wear his line of clothes, so they'd all look like him! Then, with a crackling bolt of icy magic, he had stolen the Fashion Fairies' seven magical objects and vanished into the human world.

The Fashion Fairies were horrified. They needed their special objects to make sure that everyone's clothes and accessories fit perfectly and that fashion shows everywhere were successful. Now that Jack Frost had taken the objects, all kinds of things could go wrong!

Kirsty and Rachel had been busy tracking down and returning the fairies' stolen objects, and so far they had found six of them. There was still one missing, though, and it belonged to Lola the Fashion Show Fairy.

"Here we are," said Rachel's mom.

"Wow, look at that catwalk! I can't believe you two will be walking down it in a few hours."

Rachel and Kirsty fell silent as they gazed at the scene before them. Tippington Fountains Shopping Center had opened just this week, and everything still sparkled with newness: the glass storefronts, the shiny door handles, and the magnificent fountain display. In front of the fountain was a long catwalk with rows of seats on both sides.

Kirsty swallowed, feeling nervous for the first time that day.

"I really hope we can help Lola find her magic object before the show starts," she whispered to Rachel.

"Me, too," Rachel replied, crossing her fingers. Her heart raced as she imagined all the seats filled with people watching the show. If she and Kirsty couldn't find Lola's magic object in time, it could turn out to be the worst fashion show ever!

Fairy Lights

"Hello, girls!" called a friendly voice.

Kirsty and Rachel turned to see Jessica Jarvis standing behind them. Jessica was the supermodel who had helped with the mall's fun events that week.

"I'm glad to see some more of our guest models have arrived," said Jessica, smiling.

Kirsty frowned and looked around, wondering where the guest models were — until Rachel nudged her. "*We're* the guest models." She giggled. "Jessica is talking about us!"

"Oh! Hi, Jessica!" Kirsty said, blushing.

Jessica introduced herself to Rachel's parents and promised she'd keep an eye on the girls. "I'll make sure there are some seats reserved in the front row for you," she added.

"Thank you," Mrs. Walker said, hugging Rachel, then Kirsty. "I can't wait to see you in action. Have fun!"

"See you later, girls," Mr. Walker said. "Good luck!"

Once Mr. and Mrs. Walker had left, Jessica handed special backstage passes to the girls. The passes were in plastic sleeves on long lanyards that the girls pulled over their heads.

Then Jessica took them backstage and into the dressing area. It was a large room with dressing tables, racks of outfits, and swivel chairs in front of lit-up mirrors. Dean and Layla, the other two winners of the design competition, were having their hair styled, and other models were getting makeup applied.

"Wow!" Rachel gasped, gazing around. The fashion show suddenly felt much more real, now that they could see everyone getting ready.

"I have goose bumps," Kirsty said with a rush of excitement as she spotted the scarf dress that she'd made hanging up with the other outfits. She'd  carefully stitched together lots of colorful scarves in order to make the dress, while Rachel had decorated her jeans with a rainbow pattern using glitter paint. Layla was already wearing

the stylish soccer uniform she had
designed, and Dean had on his
space-themed T-shirt
and a pair of
skinny jeans.
The hairdresser
was putting
sticky-looking
gel in Dean's
bangs and
teasing them
forward into a
space-age hairdo.

"Fabulous," Jessica said admiringly.
She turned to Kirsty and Rachel. "Girls,
why don't you change into your outfits?
Then we can talk about catwalk order.
I was wondering, since you two are

friends, if you'd like to walk down the catwalk together?" "Yes, please," Rachel said at once. She knew she'd feel much more confident with Kirsty next to her.

"That would be great," Kirsty agreed. "Come on, Rachel, let's get changed."

Jessica went to talk with Dean and Layla while the girls took their outfits to a hidden corner where they could

put them on. There was a mirror
nearby with spotlights shining all
around it. As Rachel glanced to check
that her rainbow jeans looked OK, she
noticed that one of the lights seemed to
be brighter than all the others. How
strange!

She leaned closer to investigate . . . then
gasped as a tiny fairy fluttered down
from where she'd been hiding beside
the light. *That* was why it had been so
bright!

"Kirsty!"
Rachel
whispered,
her skin
prickling with
excitement.
"Come and see!"

Kirsty finished pulling on her scarf dress and hurried over, smiling as she also saw the little fairy.

"Hello," said the fairy, landing lightly on Rachel's hand. "I'm Lola the Fashion Show Fairy. It's nice to see you two again!"

"Hi, Lola," Rachel replied, turning her body so that the fairy was shielded from view. "Have you seen your magic object anywhere?"

Lola shook her head. She had long, wavy red hair that fell around her face, and she wore a silver minidress and tall silver boots. She pointed to the pass she

wore around her neck, just like the girls'
backstage passes. The only difference
was that her plastic sleeve was empty!

"I really need to find my magical
pass before the show begins," she said,
biting her lip. "Otherwise this show —
and others like it everywhere — will
be ruined!"

Just then, Jessica called the girls over. "So, I'm going to take Dean, Layla, and the other models to the rehearsal area," she said. "I'll send someone to do your hair and makeup in a few minutes."

"Thanks," Kirsty replied politely. The other models followed Jessica, leaving the room empty except for the two friends and Lola.

Moments later, the door crashed open. Startled, Lola hid in a fold of Kirsty's dress as three boys burst in with armfuls of blue clothes, a makeup kit, and an enormous basket of accessories. The boys were all dressed alike in crazy bright blue outfits and blue hats with wide brims covering their faces.

"Move out of my way! I said, MOVE!" boomed a bossy voice. In strode a taller figure wearing a furry bright blue coat

and large blue sunglasses. "The star has arrived!" he announced with a smirk.

The air seemed to turn cold with the new arrivals, and Kirsty felt a shiver run through her as she realized who they were: Jack Frost and his goblins!

A Frosty Encounter

Rachel clutched Kirsty's arm as she also recognized Jack Frost and his goblin gang. *What are* they *doing here?* she thought in alarm, as one of the goblins locked the door behind them.

"For a start, we'll get rid of these awful clothes," Jack Frost declared, dumping the remaining outfits from the rack onto the floor. Then he carefully arranged his own Ice Blue garments in their place. "That's better."

The goblins, meanwhile, were sweeping all the makeup and accessories off the dressing tables. Powder spilled on the jewelry, lipstick smeared the pale carpet, and perfume bottles broke, releasing a mix of scents into the air.

"We won't need those anymore," said the goblins. They smirked as they unpacked the basket of makeup and accessories they'd brought — all bright blue, of course.

Lola gasped in surprise as she spotted something. "Look! My pass!" she whispered. "Jack Frost is wearing it around his neck!"

Thinking quickly, Rachel pulled Kirsty behind the rack of Ice Blue clothes before Jack Frost noticed them. They peeked out to see him easing himself into a chair in front of the biggest mirror and shouting directions to his goblins for styling his hair.

"Lola, could you please turn me and Kirsty into fairies?" Rachel whispered. "We can try to fly over and grab your pass while Jack Frost is distracted."

"Good idea," Lola replied, raising her wand. She pointed it at the girls, then waved it in an elaborate pattern, murmuring some magic words under her breath. There was a bright flash of silver light, and then a flurry of twinkling sparkles glittered all around the girls.

Seconds later, they felt themselves
shrinking smaller and smaller until they
were the same size as
Lola. Kirsty
smiled when
she saw
that she and
Rachel now
had their own
shimmering fairy
wings. She loved being a fairy!

The three friends flew carefully around
the end of the clothing rack and watched.
The goblins were busy powdering Jack
Frost's face and using hair gel to make
his long beard even spikier than ever.

"Hurry up," he snapped at them. "We
don't have all day!"

Just then, somebody tried to come into the room. "How weird. It's locked!" the girls heard from outside as the handle jiggled and turned partway. Then came a knock on the door. "Hello? Is anyone there? We came to do hair and makeup for our last two models!"

Jack Frost's top lip curled. "You're not needed anymore," he shouted. "The other models have changed their minds about appearing in my show." He cackled. "There will only be one  model today," he said in a lower voice as he spoke to his reflection. "The most handsome one in the world . . . wearing the very best clothes. Soon everyone will know it's me!"

Kirsty and Rachel exchanged a worried glance as the hair and makeup people went away. This was all going horribly wrong! But there the magic pass was, gleaming and glimmering as it hung around Jack Frost's neck. If only they could get ahold of it!

"Let's make a grab for my pass," said Lola, shooting out from their hiding place at top speed. She dove toward her magic pass, hand outstretched, but at the last moment, Jack Frost saw her in the mirror.

"Oh, no you don't!" he cried, twisting quickly so the swivel chair spun him — and the pass — out of Lola's reach.

Kirsty and Rachel tried a different approach, swooping around the back of the chair in an attempt to get the pass. But again, Jack Frost swung the chair so that it zoomed away before they could make a grab.

"Pesky fairies!" he grumbled, batting at the air with his hands. "Don't you know I have a fashion show to star in?"

Lola gritted her teeth. "It would be a better show if you gave me back my pass," she pointed out.

"No way!" yelled Jack Frost, spinning the chair around so fast that the goblins had to chase after him with the hair gel and face powder.

The fairies flew after him, too, swooping in circles as he spun the chair. He was

starting to look dizzy, Kirsty noticed. If he became much dizzier, he might not notice her grab the magic pass!

She whispered her idea to the other two, and they agreed that they'd try to make Jack Frost as dizzy as possible. Around and around they all flew, occasionally

darting in to try and grab Lola's pass, which made Jack Frost spin the chair even faster. He sagged in the chair, his face becoming as green as a goblin's. Kirsty decided that this was her best chance. She took a deep breath. It was now or never. She had to snatch the magic pass!

Mirror, Mirror

Down Kirsty flew, her eyes on Lola's magic pass. But just before she could reach it, Jack Frost suddenly staggered out of the chair and lurched across the floor. He was so dizzy that he fell into the clothing racks, knocking them over with a *crash*.

Rachel winced at the noise. Certainly someone would come and want to know

what was going on in the dressing room
at any moment! How much time did
they have before the fashion show was
going to start, anyway? Soon the
audience would be taking their seats,
anticipating a wonderful event . . . only
for Jack Frost to ruin the whole thing.
They had to stop him!

Rachel, Kirsty,
and Lola fluttered
high in the air
as Jack Frost
lunged for the
dressing-room
door, unlocked
it, and staggered
out. They
followed him

down the hallway to the curtained entrance of the catwalk.

"Excuse me, sir, you're not supposed to —" a security guard said, but it was too late to stop Jack Frost. He toppled dizzily through the curtains, grabbing them for support. Then he fell onto the catwalk, pulling the curtains down with him!

The curtain rod crashed onto
the podium and the catwalk, and the
lighting stands tipped over. Jack Frost
let out a shout of rage as he threw
the curtain off himself and sat up,
rubbing his head. He
scowled at the
goblins. "Fix
this mess —
now!" he
snapped.

The
three fairy
friends could
only stare
openmouthed
at the chaos
Jack Frost
was causing.

"If I had my magic pass, I could clean all of this up in an instant," said Lola as the crew began trying to repair the catwalk with the goblins' help. "We have to get it back before the fashion show starts. What can we do?"

Thinking hard, the fairies followed Jack Frost, who'd stomped away. The pass swung back and forth as he walked, and Rachel noticed that as he turned a corner, the pass swung out to the side. Then, seeing an empty hallway, she had an idea.

"Lola, could you use your magic to put

up mirrors all along
this hallway, and
then one at the
end?" she
asked.

Lola
nodded. "Of
course," she
said. "But why?"

Rachel smiled. "I
have an idea," she
said, and whispered it to them.

"That just might work," Kirsty said.
"And there's no time to lose. Come on,
let's try it!"

Lola waved her wand and turned
Rachel and Kirsty back into girls.
Then she waved her wand a second time,

and a whole
row of mirrors
appeared
along the
hallway, with
an extra-large
one at the end.
Now, to set the
plan in action!

"I heard that
someone from the Gorgeous Model
Agency is going to be here today,"
Rachel said in a very loud voice.
"Apparently, they're hunting for a new
supermodel."

"We should definitely practice for the
catwalk," Kirsty replied, just as loudly.
"This is the perfect spot."

The two girls began walking the length of the hallway, pretending it was a catwalk. When they reached the mirror at the end, they twirled around, causing their backstage passes to swing to the side. The whole time, they talked in loud voices about how much they hoped they'd be picked as the next supermodel. Really, they were just hoping Jack Frost would overhear them and come to find out more.

Sure enough, within a few minutes, Jack Frost appeared with his goblins. Lola, who was perched up high on a chandelier overlooking the hallway, peered down with excitement.

"If anyone's going to be picked as the next supermodel, it's *me*," Jack Frost said grandly. "Move aside, girls. Even a star like me needs to practice sometimes, and this looks like the perfect place to do it."

Jack Frost began to strut down the hallway, admiring himself. When

he reached the big mirror at the end of the hallway, the girls and Lola held their breath. If all went as planned, he would twirl around, his pass would swing out, and Lola would be able to grab it.

He began to turn, and Lola swooped down from the chandelier, her eyes fixed on the pass. This time, their plan *had* to work!

Twirl and Twirl Again

Unfortunately, Jack Frost stopped mid-twirl to gaze lovingly at himself in the mirror. This meant that his pass didn't swing out very far at all . . . and Lola had to make a quick loop and soar back to her hiding place. How horrible! Their plan was ruined again!

"Perfect," Jack Frost declared with a

smirk, as he finished his turn and headed back down the hall. The goblins watched with admiration. One even clapped!

Kirsty thought quickly. "You know, I've heard that you should do a really big, dramatic twirl at the end of the catwalk if you want the agency to notice you," she said to Rachel. "I'm going to practice that now, I think."

"No, you're not," Jack Frost told her. "Get off my catwalk, you silly girl. This is *my* practice time now, and *I'm* going to do the biggest and most dramatic twirl anyone has ever seen!"

Rachel winked at Kirsty. "*Hmmm*, I'm not sure he'll be able to do a *really* big twirl," she said uncertainly.

Jack Frost cringed with annoyance. "Well, watch this," he snapped. "Prepare to be dazzled by my twirl!"

Again, Kirsty, Rachel, and Lola all
held their breath as Jack Frost neared the
end of the hallway. Approaching the big
mirror, he whipped
around in the most
exaggerated
twirl ever,
sending his
pass flying
straight out.
In the blink
of an eye,
Lola zoomed
down at lightning speed and plucked her
pass out of the plastic sleeve. It shrank
down to fairy-size, and she flew away
with it, grinning in triumph.

Jack Frost looked so furious, Rachel
and Kirsty thought he might explode.

"That's mine!" he yelled. "Give
that back!"

"It's not yours," Lola insisted. "And
I'm using its special magical powers to
ban you from this fashion show — and
your goblins, too. I won't let you ruin
it anymore!"

Jack Frost stomped his foot, but he knew he was powerless against the magic of Lola's pass. Now that she had it back, she could use it to make all fashion shows run perfectly — which meant he was unable to stay. "Well, it's your loss," he said, sulking. "I'll go back to my Ice Castle and keep my Ice Blue designs all to myself from now on. And then you'll be sorry!"

The goblins looked pretty happy to hear this. "If you're keeping your designs to yourself, does that mean we can wear green again?" one of them asked. He lifted his blue top to reveal a green

T-shirt underneath, with GOBLINS ROCK!
embroidered in messy writing. The other
goblins cheered.

With a growling
sound, Jack Frost
stomped his
foot again,
sending a
flurry of
ice chips
swirling
everywhere.
When the ice
chips vanished,
he and the goblins
had disappeared.

Rachel and Kirsty cheered in triumph.
Then they gazed in wonder as hundreds
of bright silver sparkles began shooting

from Lola's magic pass and streaming down the hallway.

"Just in time," Lola said under her breath. "My magic will make sure the fashion show runs perfectly. Which is lucky, because it's going to start in five minutes!"

Some of the magic sparkles swirled around Kirsty and Rachel, and they gasped as their hair was magically styled and a touch of pink gloss was added to their lips. Then, as they went to look for Jessica, they saw that the catwalk had been fully repaired, the curtain was back

on its rod, and the audience members were filing in to take their seats.

"This fashion show is ready to roll," Lola said happily. "And now I should return to Fairyland and make sure that the fashion show *there* is just as perfect. Would you two like to come with me?"

Kirsty's eyes lit up immediately. She knew that time stopped in the human world while they were in Fairyland, so they wouldn't be missed for a second. "Oh, yes, please," she said, just as Rachel said the same thing.

Lola smiled and waved her wand again. "Then off we go!" she cried.

Fairy Fashions

The next moment, Rachel and Kirsty were swept up in a cloud of sparkling fairy dust and spun away from the fashion show. Soon they felt themselves land again. The sparkles cleared to reveal that they were inside the Great Hall of the Fairyland Palace. Even better, they were sitting in the front row of the audience,

next to the king
and queen of
Fairyland!

Queen Titania's
eyes twinkled as
she saw the girls.
"Perfect timing,"
she said, smiling.
"The show's about to start."

Rachel and Kirsty said hello to the
king and queen in their politest voices.
They looked around with excitement to
see the large catwalk and the huge
audience behind them.

Suddenly, the lights went down, and
the hall was plunged into darkness.
Pretty, tinkling music played and a
single bright spotlight shone on the center
of the stage as a figure appeared.

"It's Ruby!" whispered Kirsty with a
smile. She recognized Ruby the Red
Fairy, the very first fairy friend she and
Rachel had ever made.

At the beginning of the week, when
the girls had first been whisked away to
Fairyland, they had sat in this same hall
waiting to watch the fashion show. Back
then, Jack Frost had ruined Ruby's
entrance. Rachel quickly crossed her
fingers. She hoped nothing would go
wrong this time!

Ruby strode down the catwalk in a
gorgeous long red dress, edged with
glittering sequins.
She had red roses
woven through her
hair, silver bangles
on her wrist, and
red ballet shoes
with red ribbons
crisscrossing
around her ankles.

"She looks so
beautiful," said
Rachel happily.

One after another, fairies took to the
catwalk in a series of amazing outfits.
This time, there were no interruptions
from Jack Frost or his goblins, and
definitely no Ice Blue clothes to be seen!

At the end, the audience gave a huge round of applause. Kirsty and Rachel both clapped until their hands tingled! Then Lola and the other Fashion Fairies walked onstage holding hands and took their bows.

"We'd just like to say," Lola began, "that today's show would not have been possible without our friends Rachel and Kirsty — thank you, girls. Once again, you saved the day!"

A second round of applause broke out,
and the girls blushed with joy. Oh, it was
so amazing to be friends with the fairies!

Queen Titania smiled at them. "We'd
better send you back to your world now.
I can see that you have your own special
outfits to model," she said. "But before
you go, let us
give you a
sprinkling of
fairy dust,
just to make
you sparkle
even more
under the
catwalk lights."

She and King
Oberon lightly sprinkled some of their
glittering dust over the girls. "Thanks

again," King Oberon said. "And good
luck with your fashion show!"

"Good luck!" the Fashion Fairies said
at once, waving
and smiling.

"Good-bye,"
Rachel said,
waving back.
"We hope we
see you all
again soon."

Queen Titania waved her wand and
then, in a cloud of rainbow-colored fairy
dust, the girls went spinning all the way
back to Tippington.

Back at the fashion show, Rachel and
Kirsty saw Jessica coming toward them.

"There you are!" she cried. "We're
all ready to go, so come and take your

places in line. I hope you're not too nervous. I know this must all be overwhelming for you." Kirsty and Rachel grinned at each other. After seven adventures with the Fashion Fairies, outwitting Jack Frost and the goblins, and a whirlwind trip to Fairyland, the thought of walking down a catwalk actually seemed pretty relaxing!

"I think we'll be fine," Kirsty said confidently.

"That's the spirit." Jessica smiled. "I'm

going to introduce the show now, so good luck!"

Rachel and Kirsty made their way over to the catwalk entrance. Peeking through the curtains, they could see that a huge audience had gathered, including Rachel's parents in the front row.

Kirsty felt goose bumps on her arms as Jessica walked onto the stage and the audience clapped. "This is going to be great," she whispered happily.

Rachel smiled. "When we're together, things are *always* fun," she replied. "And this is the perfect way to end a very fashionable week with the fairies!"

SPECIAL EDITION

Don't miss any of Rachel and Kirsty's
other fairy adventures!
Check out this magical sneak peek of

Brianna
the Tooth Fairy!

Tooth Trouble

Rachel Walker opened her bedroom window and leaned out to gaze up at the starry sky. She took a deep breath of fresh air and smiled happily.

"This is going to be the best summer ever," she said.

Her best friend, Kirsty Tate, had arrived that morning to stay with her in

Tippington. Three long, sunny weeks stretched ahead of them. Rachel couldn't wait to find out what adventures awaited them. Whenever they were together, the most exciting and magical things seemed to happen!

She heard her bedroom door open and turned around. Kirsty came in, carrying something small in the palm of her hand.

"Rachel, guess what?" she said. "My loose tooth has finally fallen out!"

"That's terrific!" said Rachel. "We can put it under your pillow, so the Tooth Fairy can come tonight."

She closed the curtains and both girls changed into their pajamas. Then Kirsty slid her tooth under her pillow and patted it down happily.

"We've never met the Tooth Fairy, have we?" she asked, climbing under the covers. "I wonder what she's like."

Rachel and Kirsty had a very special secret. They were friends with lots of fairies and had visited Fairyland many times. Sometimes Jack Frost made trouble with his goblins. The girls had often helped the fairies foil his plans.

"Maybe we'll wake up when she comes to exchange your tooth for money," said Rachel. She got into bed and yawned.

"The Tooth Fairy is so quiet that she never wakes anyone up," said Kirsty.

Rachel smiled and turned out her bedside light. It had been a long day, and within a few minutes, both girls were fast asleep.

These activities are magical!

Play dress-up, send friendship notes, and much more!

www.scholastic.com
www.rainbowmagiconline.com

HiT entertainment

RMACTIV3

RAINBOW magic™

SPECIAL EDITION

Three Books in Each One—
More Rainbow Magic Fun!

Joy the Summer Vacation Fairy
Holly the Christmas Fairy
Kylie the Carnival Fairy
Stella the Star Fairy
Shannon the Ocean Fairy
Trixie the Halloween Fairy
Gabriella the Snow Kingdom Fairy
Juliet the Valentine Fairy
Mia the Bridesmaid Fairy
Flora the Dress-Up Fairy
Paige the Christmas Play Fairy
Emma the Easter Fairy
Cara the Camp Fairy
Destiny the Rock Star Fairy
Belle the Birthday Fairy
Olympia the Games Fairy
Selena the Sleepover Fairy
Cheryl the Christmas Tree Fairy
Florence the Friendship Fairy
Lindsay the Luck Fairy

■ SCHOLASTIC

scholastic.com
rainbowmagiconline.com

HIT entertainment

RMSPECIAL10

RAINBOW magic™

There's Magic in Every Series!

The Rainbow Fairies
The Weather Fairies
The Jewel Fairies
The Pet Fairies
The Fun Day Fairies
The Petal Fairies
The Dance Fairies
The Music Fairies
The Sports Fairies
The Party Fairies
The Ocean Fairies
The Night Fairies
The Magical Animal Fairies
The Princess Fairies
The Superstar Fairies

Read them all!

■ SCHOLASTIC

scholastic.com
rainbowmagiconline.com

RMFAIRY